"Grrr!" A scary monster ran up to Clifford. Clifford backed away. Then he saw it was Mac.

"That was scary!" said Clifford.

"Nothing scares Jetta and me," Mac said.

"Not even T-Bone?" asked Cleo.

"Not even the Ghost Dog of Birdwell Island?" T-Bone asked.

A ghost dog?

Clifford's fur stood on end. But Mac only laughed. "There's no such thing as ghosts," he said.

The movie was about to begin.

Emily Elizabeth patted Clifford.

"He has never seen a movie,"

she told Jetta.

"And this is a spooky one!"

"Nothing scares us,"

Jetta said. "Right, Mac?"

A ghost appeared

on the movie screen.

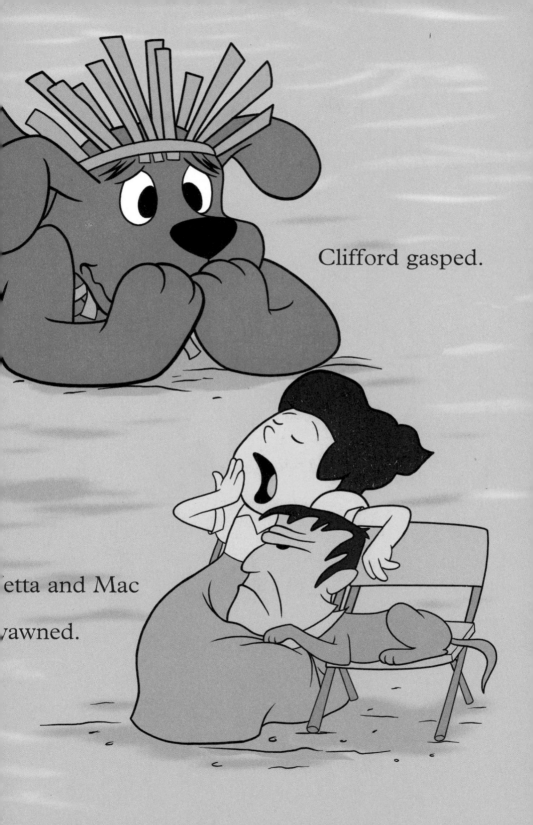

Clifford gasped.

etta and Mac

awned.

Clifford hid his eyes

for the whole movie.

Finally, he peeked out.

Emily Elizabeth was clapping.

The movie was over.

Everyone went back to town.

But Clifford stayed behind.

He wanted to know how all the
people got into the movie screen.

Clifford looked at the screen.

It was just a big white sheet.

The wind blew. *Whoosh!*

The sheet flapped.

The wind blew harder. *Whoosh!*

The sheet blew free.

It dropped over Clifford.

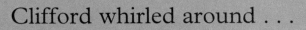

Clifford whirled around . . .

. . . and around.

What was going on?

Now he was very scared!

"That movie was fun,"

said Emily Elizabeth.

"And it was scary!"

"Humph!" said Jetta.

"It didn't scare me one bit!"

"But it's fun to be scared on

Halloween," said Emily Elizabeth.

"I've had enough of Halloween,"

said Jetta.

"Mac and I are going home."

A few minutes later,

Jetta and Mac ran back.

"Help! There's a ghost!"

Jetta yelled. "Run!"

Boom! Crash!

Something was out there.

And it was coming closer.

"It's the Ghost Dog

of Birdwell Island!"

Mac cried.

Everyone hid.

Only Emily Elizabeth stood still.

The big white ghost

came closer . . .

and closer. . . .

Emily Elizabeth stuck out
her foot.

The sheet covering Clifford
slid off.

"Why, it's not a big white ghost," said T-Bone.

"It's a Big Red Dog!" Cleo said.

"It's okay," Emily Elizabeth told

Clifford. "I'm right here."

But where were Jetta and Mac?

They were hiding under the table! Everyone gets scared sometimes," Emily Elizabeth told Jetta. "Even big brave dogs like Mac and Clifford."

"Maybe next year, Clifford can wear a sheet for Halloween," Emily Elizabeth said.

"Then he will really be Clifford, my big white ghost!"

Clifford wagged his tail.

That wasn't scary at all.

Do You Remember?

Circle the right answer.

1. Emily Elizabeth took Clifford to a movie . . .
   a. at a movie theater.
   b. at school.
   c. at the beach.

2. Why did Clifford look like a ghost?
   a. Mac played a trick on him.
   b. A white sheet fell on him.
   c. It was his Halloween costume.

Which happened first?
Which happened next?
Which happened last?

Write a 1, 2, or 3 in the space after each sentence.

The sheet falls on Clifford. _____

Everyone watches the movie. _____

Mac scares Clifford. _____

Answers:

Mac scares Clifford. (1)
Everyone watches the movie. (2)
The sheet falls on Clifford. (3)
2. b
1. c